For Joss, Mia, Matty, Molly and Aran – B.E.

For Christine – A.F.

First U.S. Edition 2002
Published by Bloomsbury, New York and London
Distributed to the trade by St. Martin's Press
Library of Congress Cataloging-in-Publication Data:
Edwards, Becky. My first day at nursery school / Becky Edwards ; Anthony Flintoft [illustrator].
p. cm. [1. First day of school--Fiction. 2. Nursery schools--Fiction. 3. Schools--Fiction.]
1. Title. PZ7
PZ7.E24983 Mye 2002 [E]—dc-21 2001043984
First published in Great Britain as *My First Day at Nursery*
ISBN 1-58234-761-1

ISBN 1-58234-761-1
Printed in Hong Kong

1 3 5 7 9 10 8 6 4 2

Bloomsbury USA Children's Books
175 Fifth Avenue
New York, New York 10010

My First Day at Nursery School

by Becky Edwards

illustrated by Anthony Flintoft

BLOOMSBURY
CHILDREN'S
BOOKS

Today is a very important day for me.
Today is my first day at nursery school.

My mom holds my hand until we get to the door of the nursery school and then she says goodbye. A friendly lady holds my hand and takes me into a great big room.

But I don’t want to be in a great big room.

I want my mommy.

There are lots of toys to play with.
There is even a playhouse with a blue tea set
and a toy store.

There are some blue
pans for cooking
and wooden
spoons for stirring.

But I don't want a playhouse or a tea set or a toy store.

I want my . . .

You can do paintings here.

There are lots of different colors and you can use sponges to paint different shapes.

There is even one in the shape of a star.

But I don't want to do painting or make different shapes.

I want . . .

You can make amazing things with the glue.

You can use shiny paper

or soft cotton balls

or bits of string.

There's even some sparkly glue,

but you have to be very careful not to get it on your fingers.

But I don't want to do
gluing or be careful

I . . .

We have a drink and cookie at nursery school

and then we sing some songs and dance to music.

There are even musical
instruments to play.
I play the drums
and the jingles.

I like the jingles best because they have lots of
shiny bells that you can shake.

There are lots of children to play with.

We run

and
jump

and chase each other all around.

It is very funny, especially when you fall down

BUMP!

and then . . .

Mom arrives to take me home.

But I don't want to go home . . .

I want to play in the playhouse
and do painting

and gluing

and play the jingles

and run around with my new friends.

I want to stay at nursery school.

Tomorrow is an important day for me.
Tomorrow is my second day at nursery school.

And I can't wait!